MEET THE GIRL TALK CHARACTERS

Sabrina Wells is petite, with curly auburn hair, sparkling hazel eyes, and a bubbly personality. Sabrina loves magazines, shopping, sleepovers, and most of all, she loves talking to her best friends.

Katie Campbell is a straight-A student and super athlete. With her blond hair, blue eyes, and matching clothes, she's everyone's idea of Little Miss Perfect. But Katie has a few surprises for everyone, including herself!

Randy Zak has just moved to Acorn Falls from New York City, and is she ever cool! With her radical spiked haircut and her hip New York clothes, Randy teaches everyone just how much fun it is to be different.

Allison Cloud is a Native American Indian. Allison's supersmart and really beautiful. But she has one major problem: She's thirteen years old, five foot seven, and still growing!

KATIE AND THE IMPOSSIBLE COUSINS

By L. E. Blair

GIRL TALK® series created by Western Publishing Company, Inc.

Western Publishing Company, Inc., Racine, Wisconsin 53404

Text by Crystal Johnson

Chapter One

"Oh, no! Katie, did I put in two cups of flour or three?" Sabrina asked me. As she scratched her head, her curly auburn hair became powdered with white flour.

"Are you guys going to take three hours to mix that dough over there?" asked Randy. She and Allison had long ago finished their job greasing the cookie sheets. Randy ate a few chocolate chips out of the bag on the counter, then licked her fingers.

"Hey, don't blame me. You know how bad Sabrina is at math — she keeps forgetting to measure each ingredient before she adds it to the mixture," I said with a laugh.

I'm Katie Campbell, and I was with my three best friends — Sabrina Wells, Randy Zak, and Allison Cloud — in the Wellses' kitchen. It's always fun to go to Sabrina's house. She has four older brothers, so there's always lots of people around, and nobody cares if you get noisy or

1

make a mess. We had come there straight after school that Monday afternoon to bake chocolate chip cookies — or at least we were trying to make them!

Sabrina remeasured the flour and then started to spoon out the sugar. "I can't believe that midwinter break is almost here already!" She sighed dramatically. Sabrina wants to be an actress someday, and as far as I'm concerned, she's perfectly suited for it.

"A whole week with no school!" Randy stretched lazily, absentmindedly popping another chocolate chip in her mouth. "I can't wait until next Monday morning. I won't have to hear my alarm clock for a whole week!"

"Aren't you forgetting something?" Allison asked her. "This year is Bradley Junior High's turn to make all the publicity material for the Main Street Fair, and the four of us got stuck with the job." Bradley Junior High is our school, and we're all in the seventh grade.

"Thanks to you, Randy, and the great job you did decorating all the school dances this year," I pointed out.

"We'll have to get together every day to make all the stuff," Allison continued. "The fair is a week from Saturday — there's no time to waste."

Randy groaned. "Those dances were a cinch. But how am I supposed to help dream up publicity material for the town fair? I've never gone to one before." Randy and her mother had moved to our town — Acorn Falls, Minnesota — from New York City last summer, after her mother and father were divorced.

"Well, I've gone to it practically every year since I was born," Sabrina said, stirring the cookie dough with a wooden spoon. "Even my parents went to the fair when they were kids. Everybody in town shows up. A brass band plays in the center of town all afternoon, and the stores on Main Street have big displays in their front windows."

Allison turned to Randy and said, "It's really fun, Randy, even if it is kind of old-fashioned. In the afternoon there's a big tent set up in Elm Park, and all the different clubs in town put on events. For instance, the Key Club holds pancake-eating races and pie-eating races — those are really funny. And the Chippewa Native American Club demonstrates our dances and traditional costumes." Allison is a full-blooded Chippewa, so her family always gets involved in that. She's basically pretty shy and quiet, but you sure wouldn't know it when she starts talking about something she's interested in.

"And there are carriage rides through Elm Park, and everybody goes ice-skating on the pond," I added. I love to skate, so that's my favorite part of the fair. "At sunset they light a big bonfire by the pond. Oh, and at the edge of the pond, people carve ice statues, and there's a prize for the best sculpture."

"Randy, maybe your mom could enter the ice statue contest!" Allison suggested. Randy's mom is an artist.

"I don't know." Randy looked doubtful. "She works in clay and papier-mâché — I don't think she's ever tried to carve ice! Besides, I can't picture M standing out in the cold all day working on a sculpture that's going to start melting the next morning!" Randy laughed. She calls her mother "M" instead of "Mom." Randy does a lot of different things!

"But the best part about the fair," Sabrina went on eagerly, "is at the end, on Saturday night, when there's a big dance in the old barn behind the lumberyard. It's like an old-fashioned barn dance, with everyone coming together —

from kids our age all the way to grandparents. You wouldn't believe how well some of those old folks can still move around the dance floor! It's a square dance — you know, with a band of fiddlers and a caller singing out all the steps."

Randy rolled her eyes. "Great!" she said sarcastically.

"I know it sounds kind of corny, but it really is a lot of fun!" Al assured her. "And we need your artistic abilities, Randy. We have to make all the posters to hang around town, plus a huge banner that stretches all the way across Main Street."

"We really want to do a good job. Everybody in town is going to see that banner!" Sabrina said.

"Oooh, all two hundred people!" Randy teased.

"Randy!" I cried.

"I'm sorry. I'm just kidding. Of course I'll help." Randy smiled.

"Finally! — we're ready to add the chocolate chips!" Sabrina carried the big bowl of cookie dough over to the counter next to the cookie sheets.

Randy looked up guiltily. "Uh ... chocolate chips?"

Sabrina's jaw dropped as she picked up the bag and peeked inside. Allison and I started to giggle uncontrollably. Randy had eaten almost the whole bag of chocolate chips!

After a quick run to the corner grocery store to replace the chocolate chips, we finally baked our cookies. Then we ate them up in half the time it took to make them! Around five-thirty my family's housekeeper, Mrs. Smith, picked me up in her big black car to go home for dinner. That was the last thing I wanted after eating a few dozen cookies!

I still miss the days when I lived in the same neighborhood as Sabrina, Allison, and Randy. I could easily walk home from their houses back when my mother and my older sister, Emily, and I lived in town. And of course, our little house there reminded me of my dad, who died three years ago. But then Mom met Jean-Paul Beauvais and fell in love with him. I was glad to see her look so happy again. Just a couple of months later, they were married, and suddenly I had a new father and a new stepbrother, Michel, who's in the seventh grade with me. Not long after that, Jean-Paul and Mom bought us a big new house on the other side of town, complete with a housekeeper, cook, and gardener! All these changes took a little getting used to, believe me.

As I walked into the foyer of my house, wondering why I had eaten so much, I heard voices in the library. I walked across the polished wood floor and through the sliding oak doors that led into the library. Mom, Jean-Paul, Emily, and Michel were all talking excitedly. They didn't even notice me in the doorway.

"What's up?" I asked. Usually only Jean-Paul uses this room, since it's attached to his home office.

"Papa just got a phone call in his office from my uncle. My Grand-mère, my cousin Noelle, and my Tante Anne and Oncle Pierre are coming for a week's holiday!" Michel announced happily. He still talks with a thick French-Canadian accent, just like his father does.

"What are we going to do, Jean-Paul?" Mom cried, looking distressed. "What day did you say they are coming?"

"Saturday. *Ma chère*, why are you so worried? It is only my mother and my sister's family — not the queen of England!" Jean-Paul teased my mother. He touched her flushed face lovingly.

"But the guest rooms aren't ready for visitors yet!" Mom sounded panicked. "We were in such a hurry when we moved in, I never got around to those three rooms. Two of them still have bare walls and no curtains — and the third one doesn't even have a bed in it yet!"

"Eileen, you got this entire house ready for us to move into in less than two weeks," Jean-Paul reminded her. "I know you are busy with your job at the bank, but that's why we hired a house-keeper. With Mrs. Smith's help, surely you can buy some pictures and curtains before Saturday. As for the third room, we don't need it. Noelle can sleep in Katie's room."

I have to admit, I gulped a little when he said that. But I couldn't think of a good reason to object to the plan. Besides, I didn't want to cause extra work for Mom.

"I guess that'll be okay," Mom said uncertainly. "But you know I want things to be just right for your sister and your mother!" She still looked nervous, and I knew why. We really didn't know Jean-Paul's family too well yet. They were all here for the wedding, of course, but they flew in the day before and left the day afterward. There were so many cousins and aunts and uncles, all speaking French half the time, I couldn't really remember who was who. But Mom tried awfully hard to know their names and talk to them all. She really loves Jean-Paul, and she wanted his family to like her, too. After all, Grand-mère is her new mother-in-law.

Jean-Paul kissed her quickly on the cheek, saying, "That's my love! Now, I must remember to send a limo to meet them Saturday afternoon. They'll be flying in on the company jet."

Jean-Paul owns the biggest advertising company in Canada, and his brother-in-law — that's Oncle Pierre — runs the Canadian office. Jean-Paul runs the Minneapolis office, which is why he moved here to Acorn Falls.

Emily said, "I think I remember Tante Anne and Oncle Pierre from the wedding. She was wearing a really beautiful long blue chiffon gown and a sapphire necklace." Trust my sister Emily to remember in detail what everybody wore, I thought. "But did we meet cousin Noelle at the wedding?" she asked. "I can't remember her."

"No, she was away at boarding school in Switzerland and couldn't make it," Jean-Paul explained.

Boarding school in Switzerland! I figured she had to be practically grown-up if her parents let her go to school so far away. "How old is she?" I asked.

"That's the best part — Cousin Noelle is our age!" Michel told me happily. "And she's really nice, too. Of course, I haven't seen her for almost two years. Even when we lived in Canada, I didn't see her because she was away at school. Sometimes she doesn't even come home for Christmas break — Tante and Oncle go to Switzerland instead, and they all take a skiing holiday together."

Well, at least the fact that she liked to ski was encouraging, I thought. If she liked other sports, too, then we would have something in common. "Great! I can't wait to meet her!" I said, trying to sound sincere. But I couldn't help wondering what I could possibly have in common with this girl.

Chapter Two

"So remember, we're all going to the mall tomorrow to buy supplies for the banner," Sabrina told me over the phone on Saturday. "Can you join us?"

I was sitting on my bed, tying my sneaker laces and talking to Sabs on my Princess phone. "I'll have to wait and see," I told her. "Jean-Paul's relatives get here today. Mom might want me to stick around this weekend."

"Why don't you bring your cousin along? She's our age, right?" Sabs suggested.

"Yes. But I'm not sure if she'll want to come," I said doubtfully.

"Why not? I don't know any twelve-year-old girl who doesn't like to go to the mall!" Sabrina cried.

I laughed. Shopping might be Sabrina's favorite pastime, but that didn't mean that it would be Noelle's. I really didn't know what a

French-Canadian girl who goes to boarding school in Switzerland would like.

"Well, I'll ask her," I promised. "I'd better go now, Sabs. Scottie and Michel are going running with me today. I want to get ready before they burst in here and complain that I'm late!"

"Running with Scottie? Oooh! How romantic!" Sabs cooed. Sometimes Sabrina likes to tease me about Scottie Silver. He and I became pretty good friends when we played together on the hockey team this season. I'm the first girl who ever joined the boys' hockey team, so Scottie and the other guys gave me a rough time at first, but by the time of the postseason playoffs they had really accepted me. I guess I do like Scottie more than a friend, but I wouldn't admit it, not even to Sabrina.

"You think running is romantic! No way! You're crazy, Sabs," I protested.

"Yeah, we'll see. Have a good time, anyway," Sabrina said sincerely.

"I'll try." I laughed. "Talk to you later!"

I hung up the phone and went over to my dresser. I put my hair up in a ponytail and inspected my reflection in the mirror. I was wearing my old gray sweatpants with thick white socks and my black-and-orange Bradley Junior High Hockey Team sweatshirt. I definitely wasn't dressed like a "lady," as my mother would say. But I was dressed just right for a good run. I would have time to shower and change before Jean-Paul's relatives got here at four o'clock.

I put on my wristwatch so I could keep track of the time. It was almost one o'clock now. Even though I felt hungry, I didn't want to eat lunch until I had finished running — a full stomach might give me cramps. Besides, I'd had a big breakfast earlier, with waffles and bacon and scrambled eggs. Jean-Paul liked to cook brunch for us on the weekends, and I think he especially wanted to do something nice for Mom today, since she seemed so nervous.

I flipped my long blond ponytail over my shoulder and trotted out the door of my bedroom. When I got to the bottom of the back staircase I could hear Michel and Scottie in the kitchen. They were hunting through the fridge, stuffing their faces with leftover chicken wings and potato salad. I swear, Michel can eat more than anybody alive!

"Hey! What are you guys doing?" I said, startling them.

Scottie Silver, tall, blond, and handsome, looked up at me and smiled. "Hi, Katie! Don't sneak up on us like that. I thought it might be your cook."

Our cook is a short stern woman who never seems to smile, except at Michel when he compliments her in French. She scares me. Luckily, she was out shopping for tonight's dinner. Normally she didn't work on weekends, but Jean-Paul had asked her and Mrs. Smith to work the extra days our houseguests would be here. Then they could have some extra time off later.

"K.C.! We needed something to eat while we waited for you to get ready," Michel teased.

"Very funny — you know I'm always on time," I told him. "That is, except when you hog the bathroom." I punched Michel playfully in the arm. Sharing a bathroom with my new stepbrother had been a hassle at first, but now we had worked things out. He was really a pretty good guy, I had to admit.

"Come on, let's get started," I said. "Michel and I have to be back by at least two-thirty to eat lunch, clean up, and get dressed. Grand-mère and Tante Anne will be here at four."

"The way you say their names, they sound

14

like Frankenstein and Dracula!" Scottie laughed.

I guess my voice showed how nervous I felt. I wasn't sure why. All I could remember about Grand-mère and Tante Anne was the elegant formal gowns they wore to the wedding, and the way they sat at their table all evening speaking French to each other. But that didn't mean they couldn't be nice. Maybe I was just picking up the jitters from my mom.

Scottie, Michel, and I walked out the front door and limbered up our muscles with some stretching exercises in the driveway. We planned to follow our usual route, down the road that our house was on. There's hardly any traffic there, and it's nice to pass by the big beautiful mansions and estates. When we got to the end of the road, we would turn and go around the outskirts of the Acorn Falls Country Club golf course. If we go around the edge of the whole course and home again, it's almost exactly three miles, a good workout.

"How about six miles today, eh?" Michel suggested.

"Six? No way!" I cried.

"Out of shape, Katie?" Scottie teased me.

"No, I just don't want to be late," I said. Then,

to show I could take a joke, I added mockingly, "If I have to slow down for you two, six miles could take two hours! It's already one o'clock."

"Don't worry, K.C.," Michel reassured me. "If it gets too late, we can cut across the course and get home faster." The golf course was closed for the winter, so sometimes we crossed the fairway to take a shortcut to our street. Jean-Paul was a member of the club, so I didn't think they would mind. Anyway, there wasn't any snow on the ground today, so no one would know if we cut across.

I could tell Scottie and Michel thought I couldn't keep up with them for six miles. But I knew I was in as good shape as they were. "Okay, you're on! But remind me to check my watch after the first time around."

They promised they would. We started off our run at a steady, reasonable pace. The cold winter air felt good against my warm face, and the good hard exercise kept me from worrying about the relatives.

After we had finished the first lap around the club grounds, I pushed up my sweatshirt sleeve to look at my watch.

"So? *Quelle heure est-il?*" Michel asked me the

time. Sometimes I think he talks French just to annoy me.

"One-thirty," I answered, puffing.

"See, we have plenty of time," Michel said. "Grand-mère won't be here until four. We can do another lap easily, and be home in time to grab something to eat." It was typical of Michel not to worry about the time it takes for a shower or to change clothes.

"Okay," I said reluctantly. "But let's hurry!" Something seemed weird to me, but the run felt so good, I didn't stop to worry. The first lap hadn't seemed to take much time. And we were probably running faster than I thought!

"Okay, Miss Athlete, you set the pace!" Scottie gasped, a little out of breath. Just to show him, I took off fast, leaving them in the dust.

Scottie and Michel shouted in protest behind me. With a grin, I slowed down, and we paced ourselves down the road.

When we had circled halfway around the golf course, I decided to check my watch again to see if we needed to take the shortcut. Funny — it was only one forty-five. We seemed to be really moving, so I didn't say anything to the guys about taking the shortcut. We were all getting tired and slowing down, but no one wanted to admit it, so we kept on running all the way around the golf course.

As we came back up the path toward the road, I pulled up my sleeve again. Then I stumbled and gasped. My watch still said one forty-five. "Oh, my gosh!" I cried and shook my wrist. But the hands did not move. The watch had definitely stopped.

"What?" Scottie and Michel both cried. They slowed down, too, and circled back to me.

I came to a dead stop, my heart pounding. "Look! My watch has stopped!" I shouted.

"Calm down, K.C.! How late could it be?" Michel asked, jogging in place.

"I don't know!" I cried. "I thought we started around one o'clock, but my watch was probably running slow even then. It could have been a lot later than that! And it must have taken us more than an hour to run six miles. We have to get home superfast!" I took off up the road, scolding myself under my breath. If I had been thinking, I would have figured out that something was wrong with my watch after the first lap. We could have gone home then, or at least we could have taken the shortcut during the second lap.

But now . . . !

I was running so hard, I had a pain in my side. I could hear Michel and Scottie struggling for breath behind me. Despite the cold, beads of sweat were starting to roll into my eyes. My ponytail began to come loose, and wet strands of hair stuck to the side of my face.

I ran down the road and raced around the hedges that lined our driveway.

Boom! I ran smack into the half-opened door of a long black limousine.

Sticking out of the door were a pair of thin legs in dark stockings and expensive-looking black pumps, waving helplessly in the air. I realized that the legs belonged to Grand-mère, who had been knocked back onto the car seat. Bracing herself against the door handle, she stared out of the car window at me, looking outraged.

A uniformed chauffeur, who had been holding the door open, rushed forward to help Grand-mère. Behind him I noticed Mom's face, completely pale, with her eyes open wide in horror. Next to her, Jean-Paul looked like he wanted to laugh, but didn't dare.

As the chauffeur helped Grand-mère shakily to her feet, I looked through the back window into the limo. I saw three heads — Tante Anne, Oncle Pierre, and someone who had to be Noelle. Then Tante Anne's head, topped with a stylish red brimmed hat, twisted around so she could peer out at me. She pursed her lips in disapproval.

Jean-Paul helped Tante Anne out of the limousine while the chauffeur walked Grand-mère toward the front steps. As Tante Anne took Jean-Paul's arm, she drew a sharp breath and said to him in her French accent, "*Mon frère* — who on earth is that uncouth girl?"

Michel and Scottie stood quietly behind me and waited.

I wished the earth would swallow me up, but it didn't. I had no choice but to hold out my hand and say, "Welcome to our home, Tante Anne. I'm your niece Katie."

Chapter Three

"Katie!" Mom said in a quivering voice. She looked like she was in shock. Emily, standing behind her, had a sort of sick look on her face, too. She, of course, was perfectly dressed in a teal blue wool skirt and a pale blue cashmere sweater and cardigan.

I pushed my hair out of my eyes and tried to wipe the sweat off my face. I had never been so embarrassed in my life.

Luckily, this whole situation didn't seem to bother Michel at all. He shoved past me. *"Grand-mère! Bonjour!"* Michel cried and hugged his grandmother hard. Then he said some more things to her in French.

She hugged him gingerly, looking him up and down with her eyebrows raised. Then she looked the same way at me. I wished once again that I could just disappear.

"Jean-Paul, *ils sont les enfants aimables, mais*

sont-ils toujours ainsi . . . bizarre?" Grand-mère spoke to Jean-Paul in French.

I listened closely but I couldn't really understand what she said. Michel only laughed. Jean-Paul smiled at his mother and shook his head. *"Non, Maman."*

Scottie, standing behind me, whispered, "What are they saying?"

"I don't know," I hissed back. But I had a good idea that it was something about me. And I knew that it wasn't very polite to speak in another language when half of the people present didn't understand it!

Next Oncle Pierre unfolded his long legs and stepped out of the limousine. He turned to help Noelle climb out, and I got my first look at my new cousin. Her outer clothing was all in winter white, from her small felt hat right down to her gloves and stockings. Her sleek blond hair was french-braided and hung neatly down her back. She looked at me for just a moment, then shyly looked away.

"There seems to be one child too many here, eh?" Oncle Pierre laughed. "Or have you added some more to your family when we weren't looking, Jean-Paul?"

22

Jean-Paul noticed Scottie standing there and laughed heartily. "*Seul un ami*, Pierre — only a friend! This is Scott Silver. He plays on the hockey team with Michel and — " Jean-Paul was about to say "Katie," but then he stopped. Maybe he knew that his sister and mother would really disapprove of a girl who played hockey!

Scottie shook Oncle Pierre's hand. "Nice to meet you, sir. But if you'll excuse me, I have to be getting on home now."

"I'll walk you to your bike," Michel quickly offered. I sure wished I had an excuse to get out of there, too.

Jean-Paul, noticing the furious looks Mom was giving me, said, "Why don't we all go inside and get out of the cold? Then Michel and Katie can get cleaned up and we can all talk over hors d'oeuvres. Wait until you taste Cook's creations — *magnifique!*" He took Grand-mère's arm and helped her up the front steps.

I breathed a sigh of relief and stood aside to let our guests go in the front door. I hoped I could stay out of sight and then sneak up the back stairs to shower.

"Katie! I don't believe you did that!" Emily hissed as she walked by and then hurried to

23

catch up with Mom.

Michel and Scottie started to giggle. I threw them an angry glare. Why was I the only one getting in trouble here? It was Michel's idea to run those extra miles.

"Did you see the chauffeur's face when Katie almost knocked your grandmother over?" Scottie snickered.

"Forget about the chauffeur — did you see her mom's face?" Michel laughed.

I scowled and spun around in a huff. As luck would have it, at that very moment I tripped over the pile of luggage the chauffeur had unloaded from the trunk. What a klutz! Michel and Scottie laughed even harder as I picked myself up and stormed inside.

I ran up the back stairs, fuming. My only consolation was that at least I would get in the shower before Michel. And once I was there, I intended to stay a long time. It would serve him right!

Once I was in the shower, I calmed down. I decided the best course would be to get out, get dressed, and go back downstairs as soon as possible. That way Mom wouldn't get any more upset than she already was. I figured she had enough to worry about without my making things worse.

When I got out of the bathroom, wrapped in my old pink terry-cloth robe, I found Noelle's matching flowered luggage, deposited by the chauffeur, in the middle of the floor. There must have been half a dozen suitcases. How many clothes did she need for one short week?

I went to my closet to pick out an outfit. I almost chose my winter-white cashmere pleated skirt, but then I remembered that Noelle was dressed in white. I didn't want to look like a clone of Noelle! Instead I settled on my dark green wool trousers with the leather suspenders. I matched those with a white monogrammed button-down blouse and my green suede flats. Then I pulled my hair back into a low ponytail with a white chiffon bow clip. I looked in the mirror and decided that I looked much better now. Maybe that would change Tante Anne's critical attitude.

I almost put on my wristwatch, then I threw it back on the dresser top. That stupid watch had been the cause of this whole mess to begin with! Instead I put on a green enamel bangle bracelet, even though it seemed kind of dressy just for dinner at home.

I trotted down the front stairs and into the foyer. I could hear Jean-Paul and his family talking in the living room. Mom calls it the parlor — I guess she thinks that sounds more formal. It is kind of a formal room, the way she has it decorated with antiques and stiff chairs. We don't go in there much unless Mom's having important company or something. When it's just the family, we relax in the family room, which has a wide-screen television, a stereo, a pool table, and big, puffy sofas and chairs. But somehow I wasn't surprised that we were using the living room tonight.

I took a deep breath and walked into the room.

"Ahh, Katie! You look very nice," Jean-Paul greeted me. He was at the small bar in the corner, fixing a drink for Oncle Pierre.

"*Oui!* Now, there is the beautiful young girl we met at the wedding!" Oncle Pierre complimented me and raised his glass.

I blushed slightly and murmured hello. Then I slipped into one of the wing chairs next to the fireplace. The crackling fire made my face hot, but I didn't want to attract attention by moving again.

Now that Noelle had taken off her winter coat, I could admire her outfit — a simple, elegant knee-length pink-and-cream-colored suit with gold buttons down the front. She sat primly on the edge of the brocaded love seat with her ankles neatly crossed and her knees pressed together. I realized I was kind of lounging in my chair, and I quickly sat up straighter and uncrossed my legs. Then I noticed that Tante Anne was looking me over from head to toe. Flushing a little, I wished I had worn a skirt after all.

Mrs. Smith carried in a silver tray of hors d'oeuvres. I was getting pretty hungry by then, since I hadn't had time to eat any lunch, but of course Mrs. Smith offered the tray to our guests first. Noelle barely glanced at the pretty little snacks carefully laid out on a paper doily. She just shook her head and said softly, "No, thank you very much." Then she delicately covered her mouth while she yawned. Well, I knew it was boring here, but I didn't think it was that boring!

Grand-mère refused the hors d'oeuvres, too. "Salty foods are not good for my blood pressure, you know," she explained.

Tante Anne peered at the tray suspiciously.

"What kind of caviar is this?" she asked. "I eat only beluga caviar."

Mom looked anxiously at Mrs. Smith. Our housekeeper, cool as ever, said, "It is beluga caviar, ma'am. The cook just opened a fresh jar." As if we had stale leftover jars of caviar sitting around the house all the time!

After Tante Anne helped herself, Oncle Pierre happily took two or three hors d'oeuvres. But I still had to wait, while the grown-ups chatted and Jean-Paul, Mom, and Emily were served. Luckily, Mrs. Smith brought the tray to me before Michel could attack it. Looking down at the tray, I couldn't even recognize the toppings on most of those elegantly decorated snacks! At random, I picked up two crackers covered with some kind of lumpy black jelly. I bit into the first one — and nearly gagged. I had never tasted such salty stuff in my life!

Then I realized that Tante Anne was watching me. "Perhaps you are not accustomed to caviar, *ma chère*," she said dryly.

I refused to let her get the better of me. "No, I really love it," I insisted. Somehow I managed to finish both crackers without making another face.

"Maman, can we see our rooms now?" Noelle asked Tante Anne in a soft, polite voice. "It has been a long day for me."

Mom jumped up, looking embarrassed. "Of course! I should have shown you your rooms right away. You must be tired from traveling and you'll want to freshen up before dinner!"

"Yes, I am fatigued. Traveling does that to me at my age," Grand-mère said. She held out her hand and waited expectantly. Oncle Pierre hurried over to help her out of the chair.

I frowned. Grand-mère wasn't that old! Besides, I knew I'd seen her get out of a chair by herself at the wedding. But then I thought guiltily, maybe she was still shaken from when I knocked her down.

"Grand-mère, I will show you to your room," Mom offered, taking her arm. "Emily, could you please show Tante Anne and Oncle Pierre to the blue room? You're all staying on the third floor — the elevator is just down this hallway."

I began to eye the hors d'oeuvre tray, hoping to scarf up something a little more edible once the guests were out of the room. But Mom turned around in the doorway. "Oh, Katie, we can't all fit into the elevator. Could you show

Noelle up the stairs to your room?" She must have felt like she had to apologize for something, because she added, "I thought it would be more fun for the girls to share a room. That way they can get to know each other better."

I dragged myself to my feet. Noelle was waiting patiently.

"Come on, my room's this way!" I tried to sound cheerful. I wasn't too excited about sharing my room for a week with Miss Perfect Manners here, but maybe once I got to know her, she'd be nice.

I bounded up the first flight of stairs and had to wait on the landing for Noelle. She was walking up incredibly slowly. I bet if I'd balanced a book on her head, it wouldn't even have fallen off!

By the next flight I was climbing slower, but Noelle was still lagging behind. At this rate, we'd never reach the top by dinnertime! "The stairs aren't so bad once you get used to them. It's really pretty good exercise," I said, trying to make conversation. Noelle smiled weakly, but she was a little out of breath and didn't say anything.

Finally we got to the third floor. "This is my room!" I announced and opened the door. I was glad that I had remembered to put my running clothes in the hamper before I went downstairs.

Noelle quietly stood and looked around.

"Your luggage is all here," I went on, still trying to be friendly. "Do you want help unpacking? You brought a lot of stuff." I was glad that my walk-in closet was still half-empty, so all of Noelle's clothes would fit.

"Oh, I do not need to unpack all my bags," Noelle said in her pretty accent. "I have just returned from Switzerland — from my school. I didn't have time to send my luggage back to our house in Montreal. I will only take out a few things for our visit here. After all, we are only staying one week. How many clothes can I wear in a week?" She gave me a shy smile.

Boy, was I relieved! I should have known there would be a logical explanation for this mountain of luggage. Besides, it was good to hear that Noelle could actually talk — and that she had a sense of humor.

"I'll wait for you downstairs," I told her. "The bathroom is through there. Oh, and make sure you lock the other door when you go in — it connects to Michel's room. You wouldn't want him bursting in on you! And the closet is in there, if you do want to hang anything up."

"Thank you. I will see you in a few minutes." Noelle waved.

As I left, Noelle was sorting wearily through a bag that was full of nothing but shoes. I turned around for a second in the doorway, and I saw her giving a huge yawn. Now I understood — she wasn't bored, she was just exhausted from the long flight from Europe. Maybe my new cousin wasn't going to be so bad after all.

And then, on my way downstairs, I remembered that I still had to sit through dinner with Tante Anne and Grand-mère. I had a sinking feeling in the pit of my stomach. These guests were going to ruin my midwinter break!

Chapter Four

The next morning, Sunday, I was still in bed when the phone rang. I wasn't asleep, though. Noelle had gotten up really early, and even though she tried to be quiet, it woke me up, too. I was lying in bed waiting for her to finish using the bathroom.

I grabbed it on the first ring and said, "Hello?"

"Good morning, Katie!" I heard Sabrina's chirpy voice on the other end of the line.

"Sabrina! Why do you sound so awake?" I groaned, glancing at the clock.

"My dog, Cinnamon, was barking early this morning and she woke me up. Then I remembered that we're meeting at the mall later, so I got up to get ready," Sabrina said cheerfully. "So, did your relatives get there all right? Do they speak English?"

I sat up in bed and tried to process all that

Sabs had just asked me. "Yes, they got here yesterday afternoon and um, yes, they can speak
English, but" — I lowered my voice, in case Noelle
could hear through the bathroom door — "it
seems like they'd rather all speak French to each
other."

I was remembering last night's dinner. Even
though Jean-Paul kept speaking in English, they
all kept talking in French. I was probably being
paranoid, but I kept feeling they were talking
about me. If they were, I guess I deserved it after
the way I met them yesterday!

"What about your cousin?" Sabs asked. "Is
she nice?"

"Yeah, I think so. But she doesn't talk much,"
I answered. In fact, throughout the whole
evening, Noelle had spoken only when she was
spoken to. But then I guess Em and I were pretty
quiet, too, since we didn't understand half of
what they were all saying. Michel, on the other
hand, never shut up the whole time. It was definitely a night I'd rather forget. I kept looking
over at Mom, with that strained smile on her
face, and I felt really sorry for her. She made an
effort to make polite conversation, but half the
time Tante Anne and Grand-mère acted like she

wasn't even there. And the worst part was that we had seven more nights just like that to look forward to!

"Is your cousin coming shopping with us?" Sabrina asked.

"I don't know — I forgot to ask her," I answered.

"Is she still sleeping?" Sabs asked.

"No, I can hear her right now, drying her hair in the bathroom," I said. "She was actually up by seven o'clock this morning!"

"She's probably still on Swiss time. They're seven hours ahead of us," Sabrina informed me. She prided herself on the fact that she always knew what time it was all over the world. She said it was because when she became an actress, she'd have to travel all over the globe. Then she would need to know the time differences so she could call her friends at a decent hour.

"Yeah, she just flew in from school yesterday, and then she had to get on the jet to come here right away. I guess it was a pretty long trip for her," I admitted.

"Gosh! She probably spent about ten hours on airplanes in one day!" Sabrina calculated. "My cousin who lives in France says it takes more than eight hours just to get to Minneapolis from France." I knew Sabrina was getting all dreamy-eyed, like she always did when she thought about living in other places besides Minnesota.

"Maybe a day at the mall will be too tiring for Noelle," I said uncertainly.

"You never know — maybe it would help her relax," Sabrina insisted. "Don't forget to ask her when she's out of the bathroom."

"I'll ask her, I promise. We're meeting at the mall at twelve, right?"

"Right. We'll wait for you in front of the pet store. I love to look at the puppies in the window," Sabrina declared.

I laughed. "Okay, twelve o'clock by the puppies."

Just after I hung up with Sabrina, Noelle emerged from the bathroom, looking beautiful. Her hair was pulled to one side and tied with a dark blue chiffon bow. She wore a navy skirt with a white blouse and a matching short navy wool jacket, with white stockings and navy patent leather flats. She definitely was ready to go out — ready for someplace a lot fancier than the Widmere Mall!

I felt like a slob in my old flannel pajamas, still in bed.

Noelle glided across the room and laid her nightgown and robe on the daybed where she had slept. Then she sat on the edge of the daybed, folded her hands in her lap, and waited.

"Good morning," I said. Somehow I felt I had to be polite.

"*Bonjour*," she answered.

"Did you sleep well?" I asked.

"*Oui*," she answered simply.

I breathed deeply and tried to think of some more small talk. Then I remembered my promise to Sabs. I said, "A bunch of us are going shopping at the mall today at twelve. Would you like to come with me and meet my friends?"

I thought I saw a spark of interest in Noelle's eyes, but she looked uncertain and said, "I must first ask my mother."

"Okay — we can ask her at brunch," I said, hopping out of bed. "Now I'd better get into the shower before Michel moves in. There's a TV over there, if you want to watch anything."

"*Merci*," Noelle said, but when I went into the bathroom, she was still sitting motionless on the bed in front of the TV.

Then, as I was about to turn on the shower, I heard the television go on very softly. I smiled. Maybe Noelle was a normal kid after all. She just hid it well under her polite, mature mask.

When I came back out, Noelle was sitting in front of the television set, absolutely mesmerized. And there was nothing on but the weather report! Maybe she couldn't figure out how to change the channel, I wondered. I must have been staring at her, because she looked up and said, "Maman doesn't let me watch any television at home. And there is no television set in the dormitory at school."

"Oh," I replied. I didn't know what else to say. I mean, Mom doesn't let me watch television unless my homework is done, but I couldn't imagine not being allowed to watch any TV at all! Tante Anne and Oncle Pierre sure did a lot of things differently in their house.

I took extra time picking out my clothes that day. I didn't want to be too dressed up for the mall on a Sunday afternoon, but I did want to look nice next to Noelle. I finally decided on my winter-white corduroy pants with a pale pink button-down blouse, my tapestry vest, and my brown suede shoes. Noelle was still sitting on the bed, now watching a rerun of "Bonanza." I figured she was waiting for me, so I wanted to hurry up. I put a cream-colored headband over my hair and I was ready to go.

Noelle and I went down the back stairs and into the kitchen, which is where the family usually eats brunch on weekends. Cook was standing scowling by the stove, with a spatula in her hand. I had forgotten she was working this weekend because of our houseguests. "Oh, um, good morning, Cook," I said to her, hoping I didn't sound as disappointed as I felt.

She answered my greeting with the usual grunt. I led Noelle through the kitchen into the dining room, where Michel, Jean-Paul, and Oncle Pierre were already planning the day. I couldn't help feeling relieved that Tante Anne and Grandmère weren't downstairs yet.

Jean-Paul set down his coffee cup. "Good morning, Katie! Hello, Noelle."

"Ahh, Katie. *Bonjour!*" Oncle Pierre turned in his seat and smiled.

"*Bonjour, Oncle Pierre!*" I said in my best French accent. I had to admit I liked Oncle Pierre. He always seemed cheerful and friendly, not stuck-up.

"*Bon*, Katie. You learn quickly," he complimented me.

"I taught her everything she knows!" Michel bragged to Oncle Pierre.

I ignored Michel and said *"Merci!"* to Oncle Pierre. Then I asked, "Where is everyone else?"

"Your mother and Emily are giving Anne and Grand-mère a tour of the house," Jean-Paul told me.

I nodded. That could take a while, since we had four floors, not including the patio and greenhouse. We even had an exercise room and indoor pool in the basement.

I poured myself a cup of freshly squeezed orange juice from the pitcher on the sideboard, and then filled my plate with a fresh-baked blue-berry muffin and a slice of ripe, juicy cantaloupe. Noelle, behind me, looked surprised that she was supposed to serve herself, but she took exactly the same things I did and followed me over to sit at the long antique dining room table.

A few minutes later, the house tour group appeared. I was glad to see that Tante Anne and Mom were chatting about the house. Maybe they were starting to get along better, just like Noelle and I were.

We said good morning to each other politely.

Then, after everyone had filled their plates and sat down, I looked at Noelle. I reminded her, "Noelle, did you ask your mom if you can come with me later?"

"*Qu'est-ce que c'est*, Noelle?" Tante Anne inquired. "What do you have to ask me, Noelle?"

Then I guess Noelle explained about the mall to her mother in French. I listened eagerly to see if Tante Anne looked like she would agree. She talked first to Noelle and then to Oncle Pierre. Then Tante Anne cleared her throat and spoke in English.

She asked my mother, "This shopping mall. It is safe, no?"

"Oh, yes! Katie goes there all the time," Mom told her, looking a little bewildered.

"I invited Noelle to come with me to the mall today," I explained to her. "Sabrina, Allison, and Randy are meeting me there. We have to buy supplies for the banner and posters we're making for the Main Street Fair next week." I wanted to make sure she knew that I had to go for an important reason. Otherwise, she might ask me to stay home and visit with our company.

"Oh, I think that's a wonderful idea! Noelle should get to meet some people her own age

41

while she's here," Mom agreed.

Great! Now the only person we had to convince was Tante Anne. She still looked skeptical, though. I couldn't figure out what she was so worried about. After all, she let Noelle fly all the way from Switzerland by herself. This was just a trip to the Acorn Falls mall!

"Come on, Anne. Let the girl have some fun," Jean-Paul told his sister.

Tante Anne hesitated for a moment and then said, "*Oui*, you can go." She added something else in French that almost sounded like a threat, and Noelle nodded soberly. But when the conversation had moved on, Noelle actually snuck me an eager little smile.

I smiled back. Somehow she made me feel like we were heading for a wild adventure. If Noelle is this excited about the mall, I thought, she'll probably go into overdrive when I take her to the Main Street Fair next weekend!

Chapter Five

"Have a good time, girls!" Emily called out the car window as she left Noelle and me at the mall entrance just before noon.

As we walked in through the big glass doors, the mall looked really crowded — probably because it was the first weekend of midwinter break. Noelle's eyes popped wide open and she looked around at everything like she'd never been in a mall before. Come to think of it, maybe she never had!

"Let's go upstairs and meet my friends," I told her. The pet store that Sabrina loved so much was on the second level.

Noelle nodded and followed me up the escalator. It was kind of fun showing her around, even though she didn't talk much!

I spotted Sabrina's curly red hair at the end of the mall and hurried toward her. If anybody could make Noelle talk, it would be Sabs. I remembered how quiet Allison used to be when we first met her at the beginning of this school year. But now that she was best friends with Randy, Sabs, and me, she was hardly ever shy anymore!

Randy and Allison saw us first and waved. Sabrina, of course, had her nose pressed against the glass window, cooing at the puppies.

"Hi, guys!" I said. "This is my cousin Noelle. Noelle, this is Sabrina, Randy, and Allison."

Noelle nodded her head to each one and said, *"Bonjour."*

Sabrina, turning away from the puppies, gushed, "Oohh, you speak such beautiful French! I wish I could — it's such a romantic language. I have a cousin who lives in France." Then she grabbed Noelle's hand and pulled her over to the window. "You have to see this one puppy. He is so adorable!"

Noelle allowed herself to be led to the window. Then she smiled and laughed as the puppy rolled playfully out of his bed and into the food dish.

"He looks just like my dog, Cinnamon, when she was little," Sabrina told Noelle. "Do you have any pets in Canada?"

Noelle shook her head. "No. Maman is allergic." She looked back at the puppy longingly.

"Don't feel bad, I didn't have a pet until recently," Randy said. "But I made sure I got a kitten so I wouldn't have to get up early every morning to walk a dog in the snow!"

"Randy just moved here from New York City. She's not used to the cold yet," I explained to Noelle.

She nodded and smiled. "You should feel the cold in Canada and in Switzerland!"

I felt pleased. I knew my friends could bring Noelle out of her shell.

"We'd better get to the art store and buy our supplies," Allison reminded us gently.

"Oh, I almost forgot." Sabrina finally dragged herself away from the window.

We were in and out of the art store in a jiffy, with Randy's help. The fair's treasurer had given us twenty dollars for supplies, and it was just enough to get everything we needed for the banner and posters.

Then we had time for fun shopping. Sabrina pulled Noelle all through her favorite clothing store, Dare. Noelle seemed to liked some of the clothes, which kind of surprised me. Nothing in

Dare looked like the expensive, dressy clothes I had seen Noelle wearing so far. But maybe that's why she liked the stuff Sabrina showed her — it was different.

As we walked past the video arcade, Randy tugged on Noelle's arm. "We have to go in here!" Randy said. "You can't visit America and not play Mario Brothers!"

Noelle hesitated. "I don't know how."

"Don't worry, you'll catch on," Randy reassured her. "I'll play first and then you play. I'll help you!" Before Noelle had a chance to protest, the quarters were popped into the machine and the music had begun to play.

"Okay, now watch. This stick moves the direction of your guy and this button makes him jump in the air," Randy explained.

Noelle watched carefully and giggled a few times at the little cartoon man on the screen.

I glanced around the arcade to see who was there. There were always kids from our school around this place. I spotted Scottie and some of the hockey team, playing a car race game.

I waved and they waved back. Then Scottie called me over. Noelle seemed all wrapped up in watching Randy play, so I walked over to Scottie.

"Hi," I said to the guys.

"Hey, K.C.!" said Flip, one of the guys on the team, while keeping his eyes on the video game he was playing.

"Whoa! Katie, you have to introduce me to that girl you're with," said Brian, an eighth grader who plays left wing, the same position as me. He was staring at Noelle.

"Listen, Brian, hands off! That's Michel and Katie's cousin," Scottie warned him.

"Okay, chill." Brian stepped back. "Touchy, touchy!"

I smiled at Scottie. Sometimes he seemed like a big brother, the way he was so protective!

"Did you get in major trouble yesterday?" he asked me.

"No, nobody said a thing about it. At least, not in English," I added.

Scottie nodded. "Cool! It wasn't really your fault anyway, the way you bowled over your grandmother."

Scottie started to smirk and then broke out laughing. I tried to hold it in, but then I had to laugh, too. It must have been quite a sight, the way Michel, Scottie, and I had come charging up that driveway.

"So, where are you guys going next?" Scottie asked.

"The pizza place, I think. Sabs is trying to cram every American tradition into one day for Noelle," I told him, rolling my eyes.

"Noelle? Is that her name?" Brian pricked up his ears. Scottie glared at him, and Brian defended himself. "I was just asking! Lighten up!"

"We'll see you at the pizza place, then. Save us a table," Scottie told me.

"Definitely!" Brian agreed, still watching Noelle.

When I got back to Randy, Noelle, Sabs, and Allison, Noelle's man had just gotten captured and the game was over, but she really seemed to have enjoyed herself. Smiling and talking to Randy, she looked like a totally different person.

I suggested that we go over to the pizza place for a slice and a soda. When we got there, it turned out that Sabrina's twin brother, Sam, and his friend Nick Robbins were already there.

"Great! We can sit at Sam's table," Sabrina decided. Even though she seems to have a crush on someone new every week, I think Sabs has always had a thing for Nick.

"I hope it's a big table. Scottie, Brian, and Flip

are going to join us, too," I warned.

"No big deal. We can all squuush in." Sabs waved her hand airily.

"Squuush?" Noelle asked, frowning.

"Yeah, squeeze in. You'll see." I laughed. We'd have to teach her some American slang!

We walked to the back of the pizza place, where Sam and Nick had saved a booth. Luckily, it was pretty big and we could pull chairs up to it for Scottie, Brian, and Flip. It would still be a tight squeeze, but I didn't think anyone would mind.

While Randy and Allison and I went to the counter to order us two large pizzas with all the works, Sabrina introduced Noelle to Sam and Nick. By the time I got back to the table, they were asking her all kinds of questions about where she lived and where she went to school.

In her quiet voice and pretty accent, Noelle answered all the questions, and I learned some more about her myself. I found out that she learned to ski when she was about three, and she likes it a lot — except when her mother makes her take private lessons. She said she prefers to ski by herself, on freshly fallen snow with no one around. I understood just how she felt. My favorite thing is to skate alone outdoors on the pond in Elm Park when the ice is smooth as glass and I have it all to myself.

"Are the guys at your school cute?" Sabrina asked. I swear, sometimes she has a one-track mind!

"There are no boys there. I go to a girls' school," Noelle told her.

"A girls' school! Yuck!" Sabrina cried. Then she apologized quickly. "I'm sorry, Noelle. I'm sure it's a neat school, but I just can't imagine not having any guys around." After all, Sabrina lived with four brothers.

Noelle smiled. "It's not so bad."

We had just started in on our pizza when Scottie, Brian, and Flip joined us. If Noelle had seemed shy before, she was supershy once all the guys were there.

Brian tried to smile at Noelle, but she looked down as if she hadn't even seen him. I guess Brian is pretty cute — a lot of the girls at Bradley like him. I never thought of him like that, though, because we're on the hockey team together, and besides, sometimes he acts kind of stuck-up. But today he was being really nice to Noelle. "How long are you visiting for?" he asked her.

Still looking down at her lap, Noelle answered in a tiny voice, "We leave Sunday."

Brian flirted some more. "So that means you'll be around for the dance on Saturday?"

Noelle looked up at me. "Dance?"

Sabrina, who loves to play matchmaker, jumped right in. "Yeah, they have this big barn dance at the end of the Main Street Fair on Saturday. It's like the grand finale to the fair. We're all going, and all the guys will be there, too — right?"

Brian answered quickly, "Oh, I'll definitely be there! Right, Scott?" Brian elbowed Scottie in the ribs.

"Right," Scottie answered wearily, rolling his eyes. I had to laugh at Brian. I had never seen him so infatuated before.

Eventually the boys all started talking about basketball, and we girls tried to plan out our posters for the fair. With the guys there, though, it was hard to discuss anything seriously. Finally we decided to meet the next day to work at Sabs's house. Thank goodness it was midwinter break!

By the time Mrs. Smith came to pick up Noelle and me, I was feeling pretty happy. It was kind of fun having Noelle around, I thought. But then I remembered that Tante Anne and Grand-mère were waiting for us at home, and it was like a black cloud drifting in to block out the sunny day.

When we got home, Noelle and I shot right up to my room to dress for dinner. I waited to see what she was wearing before I chose my outfit. Noelle put on a mustard-colored wool skirt and an olive green angora sweater.

I put on the outfit I almost wore last night — a winter-white cashmere pleated skirt with a white silk blouse trimmed with gold braid. I figured that if Tante Anne approved of Noelle's white outfit yesterday, she wouldn't disapprove of my wearing something similar tonight.

When we walked down the stairs, we found everyone else already in the living room. "Ahh! Here are the girls! Let's go on into dinner!" Jean-Paul smiled at me.

Once we were all seated at the large dining room table, Mrs. Smith served us our salads. I was relieved to notice that everyone was speaking English tonight.

"Noelle, did you have a nice time today with Katie?" Oncle Pierre asked cheerfully.

"*Oui*," Noelle answered sincerely and smiled at her father.

"And what did you do all day?" Tante Anne asked.

Noelle picked at her food and answered, "We bought some art supplies for the banner."

"And that took three hours?" Tante Anne asked.

Noelle didn't answer, so I jumped in.

"We had a great time! You should have seen her, Tante Anne. She played video games, and then we ran into some of the guys from school and we all shared a pizza!" I told them.

Tante Anne's eyebrows flew up. "Guys?" She looked down her nose, first at Noelle, and then at me. I felt almost as if her eyes were darting deadly rays at us!

Then Grand-mère said, "Video games? What a useless waste of time! You could ruin your eyesight — and I dare say you will ruin your figure, too, Noelle, if you continue to eat pizza!" Grand-mère said all this in such a matter-of-fact tone of voice, it was impossible to contradict her without being downright rude.

"*Oui, Grand-mère*." Noelle's face fell. Her mother began to say something to her in French,

53

but Oncle Pierre quickly cut in. "I think it sounds great, Noelle. It's about time you did something fun with normal twelve-year-olds." It sounded like Oncle Pierre was actually speaking more to Tante Anne than to Noelle.

Tante Anne snorted, but she held her tongue. In fact, she was silent as a stone for the rest of the night. In one way, that was a relief. The problem was that Noelle was awfully quiet, too — even quieter than she had been yesterday evening. The general atmosphere was pretty chilly. Only Mom chattered away, trying hard to keep a pleasant conversation going. I felt sorry for her, and I was glad when dinner was over.

Noelle excused herself right after dinner, saying she still had jet lag and needed to go to bed early. I was going to offer to go upstairs with her, but Mom shot me one of her you'd-better-be-nice-to-company looks. Gritting my teeth through the stilted after-dinner conversation in the living room, I tried to think how I could help poor Noelle. Then I had a brainstorm.

I waited until Tante Anne had left the room to help Grand-mère up to bed. Oncle Pierre and Jean-Paul were sampling some of Jean-Paul's favorite French cognac, which he brought out only on special occasions. I figured now was as good a time as any. "Oncle Pierre," I asked innocently, "would it be all right with you if Noelle came with me tomorrow to help make the banners and posters for the fair? We'll be working at my friend Sabrina Wells's house. It'll just be me, Noelle, and Sabrina, plus the other two girls on the committee."

Oncle Pierre smiled his usually hearty smile. "But of course, Katie!" he said in his booming voice. "I am so glad that you girls are getting along so well."

"Thanks a lot," I said, feeling triumphant. I was determined that Noelle was going to have a good time on this vacation, in spite of her mother!

Chapter Six

The next morning I lay in bed a few extra minutes, enjoying the feeling that I didn't have to rush off to school this Monday morning. Noelle came out of the bathroom, a towel wrapped around her wet hair. "Don't bother to get dressed up today," I announced, bouncing out of my bed. "You can borrow one of my old sweatshirts and some jeans — I don't want you to mess up any of your good clothes. We're going to Sabs's house to paint posters!"

Noelle looked startled. "But I have to ask Maman, first!"

"Don't worry about that," I told her. "After you went to bed last night, I asked your father if you could go. He said yes."

"Katie! You didn't!" Noelle cried in horror.

"Don't you want to come?" I asked, surprised.

"No — I mean yes, I want to come, but . . .

what did Maman say?" Noelle frowned.

"I don't know. I asked your father when your mother wasn't there. But he said you could definitely go!" I told her.

Noelle looked skeptical but hopeful at the same time. "I will ask again," she finally decided.

"Okay, but let's ask right away. I'm sure your dad is with Jean-Paul in the dining room, eating breakfast before they go in to the office together. There's no time to lose — we have to be over at Sabs's around ten," I said. I grabbed her arm and pulled her toward the door.

Noelle looked doubtfully down at her bathrobe. "Go downstairs like this?"

"Sure, why not?"

Noelle followed me downstairs, though her feet were dragging on every step. Oncle Pierre and Jean-Paul were in the dining room, as I had hoped. But unfortunately, Tante Anne and Mom were there, too. And from the way Tante Anne's lip curled, I gathered that she did not like seeing Noelle downstairs in her bathrobe — much less seeing me in my old flannel pajamas!

Suddenly Noelle froze up beside me. Mom frowned, obviously wondering why we weren't dressed. "Katie, haven't you forgotten something?" she asked.

"I'm sorry, Mom," I said. "But Noelle wanted to ask her father about something before he left."

Oncle Pierre smiled encouragingly. "Well, *ma chère*, what is it?"

"It's about today . . . about going to Katie's friend Sabrina's house . . ." Noelle began hesitantly.

Tante Anne's back stiffened. "I do not believe I was consulted about this plan." She glowered.

"I asked Oncle Pierre last night and he said it would be all right!" I pleaded.

Tante Anne shot Oncle Pierre a withering look. "That is all very well. But, Pierre, you did not take into account the plans that Eileen and I have made for today." She exchanged significant glances with my mother.

Mom cleared her throat. I could tell she was uncomfortable, but Tante Anne was practically forcing her to take sides. "Well, we were talking about taking the girls over to the country club for luncheon today. But it's not as if we couldn't rearrange our schedules. . . . "

I knew that Mom had only been able to get a couple of days off from the bank to show Jean-Paul's relatives around town. But why hadn't she warned me that I was expected to help entertain today? I'd already told her I had to help with the fair publicity stuff, even though I hadn't exactly told her that we were doing it today. And I was taking Noelle with me, so didn't that count as "being nice to company"?

Jean-Paul must have noticed Tante Anne's expression. If she had been a cartoon character, I swear she would have had puffs of steam coming out of her ears! For once, Jean-Paul caved in.

"Katie, I think you and Noelle had better go with Mom and Tante Anne today. Perhaps you can help the girls tomorrow. After all, the fair is not until Saturday, no? Surely there is plenty of time."

"But we have to put the posters up before the fair," I protested. "So people will know about it ahead of time!"

Mom couldn't help smiling. "Katie, Acorn Falls has been having that fair during midwinter school break every year for the past forty-eight years," she reminded me. "I'm sure everybody will be glad to see your posters up around town, but I think most people are already planning to be there."

I could see there was no way out of this.

Reluctantly, I went back upstairs to call Sabrina and tell her we couldn't come.

"No sweat, Katie," she assured me. "Randy and Al and I can do the posters today — we already discussed yesterday just what to put on them. Maybe tomorrow you and Noelle can help us hang them up around town. And as far as the banner goes, that doesn't have to be done until Friday, when the workmen are going to hang it up. Maybe you guys can come over and work on that someday later in the week."

"Thanks for understanding, Sabs," I said, and hung up. But I still felt bad for letting my friends down. And I felt even worse for Noelle. She looked so disappointed, sitting on her bed watching me. I hadn't realized how much she had wanted to spend the day with me and my friends.

The lunch at the country club was a real drag, just as I had expected. I didn't see anybody I knew, which was no surprise, since we hadn't gone there very often. Jean-Paul joined the club only recently. The carpeted dining room was so hushed, I almost felt afraid to talk out loud. And practically everything on the menu was what I think of as "old-lady food" — fussy salads and little sandwiches cut in triangles. I did find a hamburger on the menu, but even that came neatly cut in half and held together with toothpicks that had little gold plastic flags embossed with the club shield!

The whole time we were sitting there, all I could think about was how much fun Sabrina, Randy, and Allison were probably having right that minute.

Luckily, that night Jean-Paul and Mom took Grand-mère, Oncle Pierre, and Tante Anne out to a fancy restaurant for dinner. We kids were allowed to stay home, and Cook made us sloppy joes and french fries. Usually such "low cuisine" was beneath her, but Michel talked her into it. And Mrs. Smith even let us eat dinner off trays in the family room. I guess we deserved it, after all the formal meals we'd sat through lately.

Later that night, I was sitting up with Emily watching the end of a movie on TV when the grown-ups came home. While the others went up to bed, Jean-Paul sat downstairs with us. After the movie ended, he asked me to stay for a minute when Emily went up to bed.

"Katie, I wanted to thank you for going

along with the plans today," he said kindly. "I know you would rather be with your best friends. But as you may have noticed, my sister Anne can be a very difficult person when she is crossed."

I nodded. Actually, I thought she could be a difficult person even when she wasn't crossed, but I didn't want to say that to Jean-Paul. She is his sister, after all.

"You see, when my sister and I were very young, our family didn't have much money," he explained. "For me, those were happy days, because I was still young and didn't care. But Anne was older, and it hurt her that she couldn't have nice clothes or go to a fancy school. So when my father became successful, Anne began to put on airs and act as if we'd always been rich." I tried to imagine Tante Anne as a girl my age, envious of the things other girls had. I couldn't quite see it, but then I didn't know her as well as Jean-Paul did.

"I'm afraid that wealth and social position mean a great deal to Anne." Jean-Paul sighed. "Maybe that's why I appreciate so much that your mother doesn't really care about things like that. I have seen how unhappy people can be when they start to think that having money makes them better than other people."

He patted my knee and smiled gently. "You have a good heart — *un bon coeur*, Katie. I know I can count on you to be understanding." I smiled back at him. Somehow, I didn't mind so much when Jean-Paul spoke in French.

After what Jean-Paul had told me, I tried not to argue the next day when Mom and Tante Anne announced their plans for the day. This time Noelle and I were expected to go with them and Grand-mère into Minneapolis to visit a couple of art museums. I don't have anything against art, but I knew that the fair posters had to be hung up today. I had to call Sabrina and apologize once again. She said she understood, of course. But that wasn't the point. The point was that I had been looking forward to running all over town taping up the posters on lampposts, on empty walls, and in store windows. It would have been a lot of fun.

I guess Mom could tell that I didn't enjoy myself on Tuesday, either. I just sat in the backseat of the car with Noelle, staring glumly out the window. Throughout the day, I only bothered to speak when I was spoken to. Now I knew why Noelle was usually so quiet!

Anyway, Wednesday morning at breakfast, Mom said that she was taking Tante Anne and Grand-mère shopping, and Noelle and I could do whatever we liked. I tried not to look too thrilled! As soon as I could, I ran upstairs and called Sabrina. "Are you guys planning to work on the banner today?" I asked breathlessly.

"Sure," she replied. "Randy and Al were going to come over in about half an hour. Can you actually come over and help today?"

"Yes!" I told her.

"What about Noelle? Will they let her join us?"

"Gee, I forgot to ask," I said guiltily. "I was just so glad that I could get away. . . . "

Then I looked up and saw Noelle standing in the doorway of our bedroom. Her eyes were shining and she was nodding her head eagerly.

"Yep," I said happily. "Noelle will be there, too."

Mrs. Smith drove us right over and we were soon knocking on the back door of Sabs's big white house. Sabrina answered the door and excitedly pulled us into the kitchen.

"Hi, Katie, hi, Noelle! We started on some

sketches for the banner. They're great!" she cried. Her red hair was pulled back in a ponytail and she wore an old blue shirt that must have been her father's, since it hung way down to her knees.

"Hey, guys!" Randy called to us from the kitchen table.

She, of course, was dressed in black, which is her favorite color.

Noelle was busy petting Sabrina's dog, Cinnamon, who had already gotten one big dirty footprint on her pants. She tried to wipe off the footprint. "Don't worry," I assured her. "Those old jeans of mine you're wearing are such a mess already."

"Come see the sketch Randy made for the banner!" Allison called out. "All we have to do now is decide which colors should go where on the real thing."

I couldn't help feeling a little left out, seeing that Randy and Al and Sabs had already gotten so far along without me. But soon it didn't bother me, once we were all sitting at the table hard at work.

After a couple of hours, we decided to take a break. Sabrina found a bag of taco chips, and we all helped ourselves to sodas from the fridge. That's the way things are around the Wellses' house — you just kind of make yourself at home right away. Even Noelle did!

"Oh, Noelle, let me show you my bedroom. Come on upstairs!" Sabrina cried and led the way up to her attic bedroom. It was two flights of stairs, and I was ready for a slow walk up behind Noelle. When she suddenly bounded the stairs, I stood there in shock. Boy, Noelle was a totally different person while she was with my friends. And then I realized that it wasn't just being with my friends that did it — it was being away from her mother!

Sabrina's room had the usual lived-in look, with clothes hanging out of the drawers and her schoolbooks on the floor. It was still a nice room, though, with a soft white bedspread, a pretty white dresser, and posters hanging on the walls. "I like your room very much!" Noelle told Sabs sincerely.

Sabrina smiled. "You really do? Thank you, but I bet it's not half as nice as yours must be."

Noelle shrugged. "My room isn't so nice. I have very nice furniture that Maman bought me, but I didn't get to pick it out myself. And I have no pictures like yours on the walls," Noelle explained. "It doesn't matter, though. I am hardly ever at home. I live mostly in Switzerland, and there I have two roommates."

"That must be fun!" Allison said. "Almost like having two sisters."

Noelle kind of shrugged and nodded at once.

"So, Noelle! You are coming to the dance Saturday night, aren't you?" Sabrina asked. I could see the matchmaker look in her eyes.

"*Oui,* I hope to. I must first ask Maman," she answered.

"Well, I'm sure she'll let you go. It'll be your last night here!" Sabrina said. I raised my eyebrows. I wasn't so sure Tante Anne would let Noelle go.

Noelle was quiet.

"We definitely have to plan what you're going to wear that night. You want to look nice for Brian, don't you?" Sabrina said with an innocent look on her face.

Noelle blushed and then giggled. "He is nice, no?"

"Very nice!" Randy smiled.

"And cute!" Allison agreed, smiling at Noelle, too.

Noelle got even redder. "Okay, guys. Stop embarrassing Noelle," I ordered.

"It is all right, Katie. I think he is cute, also," Noelle admitted.

"I knew it!" Sabrina cried.

"It is fun being friends with boys," Noelle said shyly. "I don't know many boys that well. We have dances sometimes with a boys' school near mine in Switzerland, but you don't get to know anyone very well at such formal affairs. You are all lucky to have such nice friends as Scott and Brian and Sam and Nick." Noelle giggled as she tried to remember all the guys' names.

"Yuck! Sam isn't a friend, he's my brother!" Sabrina said, rolling her eyes. "You wouldn't think it was fun to have four brothers like I do — believe me!"

Once we'd finished the tour of the house, Sabrina led us down to her basement, where we would be painting. Sabrina's father owns a hardware store, and he had donated a long piece of stiff canvas for the banner. It was already laid out on the basement floor.

It took us almost an hour to carefully pencil in the letters that spelled out ACORN FALLS 48TH

ANNUAL MAIN STREET FAIR. Then we got out small pots of paint in the colors that had been chosen for this year's fair: spruce green and ice blue. This was my favorite part. I loved painting, although I got more paint on myself than on the banner.

In the beginning Noelle was being supercareful not to get dirty. She barely got one letter painted in an hour! But after Sabrina accidentally dropped her paintbrush on Noelle's leg, Noelle loosened up. By the end of the day she was as covered in paint as we were.

We finished the banner and hung it up in Sabs's basement. It looked great, if we did say so ourselves.

Noelle and I got home with just enough time to get cleaned up for dinner. As we came in the front door, I started to laugh. "What is it, Katie?" Noelle asked, smiling.

I steered her over to the foyer mirror. "Look — you've got a big glop of blue paint in the back of your hair!"

Noelle started to laugh, too. "That is nothing. Look at the green paint in your ears! And your hands are almost totally blue!"

We both doubled up laughing. We barely

heard the firm footsteps coming down the stairs. *"Noelle! Mon Dieu!"* Tante Anne's stern voice interrupted us. That killed our laughter pretty fast, believe me.

Noelle spun around and quickly started to apologize to her mother. But Tante Anne cut her off abruptly, saying something in French that didn't sound at all nice.

Before I knew it, Noelle was slowly walking up the stairs with her head hanging down — and Tante Anne was giving me a look that could kill!

Chapter Seven

Katie dials Sabrina.

SABRINA: Hello?

KATIE: Sabrina, it's Katie. I'm sorry to bother you — I know you're probably still eating dinner.

SABRINA: Don't worry about it, we're done. What's the matter? You sound upset.

KATIE: I am. Something terrible happened, and I feel like it's my fault.

SABRINA: Ohmygosh! What?

KATIE: When we got home, Noelle's mother saw us all covered with paint, and we were laughing hysterically. Tante Anne really blew her top and said something to Noelle.

SABRINA: What did she say?

KATIE: I couldn't understand it, because she was talking in French, but it made Noelle really upset. She didn't even come down to dinner. And when I got back to my room after dinner, she had moved all of her stuff out of my room and into Grand-mère's bedroom! Her mother doesn't want me around her anymore.

SABRINA: That's silly, Katie. You're the nicest girl around. Why would anyone's mother not like you?

KATIE: I'm not just imagining things! Michel overheard Tante Anne saying to Jean-Paul that I was a bad influence on Noelle. And now Noelle isn't allowed to go to the fair or the dance.

SABRINA: That's so rude! Poor Noelle — we have to do something! Let me talk this over with Randy and Allison, and I'll get back to you, okay?

KATIE: Okay, thanks.

Sabrina calls Randy.

RANDY: Yo!

SABRINA: Hi, Randy. It's Sabrina. Katie needs

our help.

RANDY: Sure, what's up?

SABRINA: Noelle got in big trouble with her mom for getting all dirty today. And now she's not allowed to hang out with Katie. She's not even allowed to go to the fair on Saturday, let alone the dance. And that's her last chance to see Brian!

RANDY: Well, you have to admit, her mom has a point. We were all covered with paint. I mean, if M wasn't an artist, she probably would have gone ballistic when I got home and she saw me, too.

SABRINA: That's probably true, but it sounds like Noelle's mother is beyond mad — she sounds freaked out. Katie's really worried. I think we should go over and apologize to Noelle's mother. I mean, I was the one who first dropped my paintbrush on Noelle's jeans.

RANDY: Maybe she didn't know that Noelle was wearing Katie's jeans. Or maybe she didn't realize that that paint is totally washable. I'll bet she calms down when she gets the whole story.

SABRINA: I don't know — she doesn't sound like that kind of person. Poor Noelle is never allowed to have any fun, not even on her vacation. I think we should try to help her! Let me call Al and see what she says.

RANDY: Okay, but if I were you, I'd just cool it for a few days.

SABRINA: But it's already Wednesday night, and the fair is on Saturday. By the time her mother comes around, it could be too late! I'll call you later.

Sabrina dials Allison.

ALLISON: Hello, Cloud residence. (*Sound of a baby crying in the background.*)

SABRINA: Al, it's Sabs. I have to talk to you.

ALLISON: Oh, Sabs. It's a really bad time. My parents went out to dinner; our sitter, Mary, is at the library studying for an exam; the baby is screaming, and she just spit up all over me!

SABRINA: Yuck! I'm sorry, but I really need

your advice.

ALLISON: Hey, I know! Give me ten minutes to calm everything down and I'll call you right back, okay?

SABRINA: Great! Talk to you soon.

A few minutes later, Allison calls Sabrina back.

ALLISON: Okay, I've got things under control. Thank goodness the baby always stops crying when Charlie plays with her. So, what's up?

SABRINA: I need your advice. Noelle's mother got really angry at Noelle today because she got paint all over herself. Apparently she thinks Katie is a bad influence on her. She made Noelle move out of Katie's room, and now Noelle can't go to the fair.

ALLISON: That's really strange. Just because she was dirty? Are you sure it wasn't something more than that? I mean, maybe she came over to your house without permission, or something like that.

SABRINA: I don't think so. I want to go talk to her parents and explain why we were dirty and how much fun the fair will be.

ALLISON: I don't think you should, Sabs. If Noelle's having problems with her parents, she's the one who has to talk it out with them.

SABRINA: Well, I think I'm going to try.

ALLISON: Maybe you should ask Katie first. If you make them mad, for sure they'll blame it on Katie, too, since you're Katie's friend.

SABRINA: Okay, but I'm going to talk it over with Katie tomorrow. And if things aren't better with Noelle, I'm going over there! I'll see you tomorrow.

ALLISON: Sure, bye.

Chapter Eight

On Thursday morning I felt sad when I saw Noelle's empty bed and remembered what had happened. And when I saw Noelle at breakfast, she sat silently gazing down at her lap and refused even to look at me!

Now that Tante Anne was determined to keep Noelle away from me, I wasn't asked to join their plans for that day. I was glad to be free to hang out with my friends again, but I sure didn't like the reason why I was free.

That afternoon I went skating with Sabrina and we discussed the Noelle situation. We both agreed that we should try to change Tante Anne's mind, at least to let Noelle come to the fair and the dance.

Sabrina wanted to help in the name of romance. She thought that Noelle and Brian were destined to fall in love at the dance. I wanted to help Noelle stand up to her mom for a bigger reason. I had seen what a fun, outgoing person she could be when Tante Anne wasn't around. I felt like I had to help Noelle break away from her mother's strict rules, or else she'd be doing what her mother wanted her to do for the rest of her life. And I knew that would never make her really happy.

When I got home that afternoon, I heard noises in the family room and looked in, hoping that it was Michel. I had to talk to someone about how horrible I felt. I couldn't talk to Mom about it — this week was hard enough on her, trying to entertain her new in-laws.

"Hey, Katie. What's up?" Reed, Emily's boyfriend, greeted me when I walked through the sliding wood doors.

He was playing pool and Emily was sitting on the sofa, watching.

Reed is really cute and he's a nice guy, too, which is a combination hard to find sometimes. He and Emily are both in high school together and they make the perfect "Ken and Barbie" couple. In fact, they even look like Ken and Barbie. Emily has long slim legs, blue eyes, and beautiful long blond hair. Reed has wavy sandy brown hair, hazel eyes, and broad strong shoulders and arms. Emily is the captain of the pom-pom squad and Reed is captain of the basketball team. They both get really good grades and are basically so perfect together that it almost make me sick sometimes!

"Hi," I answered, and then I turned to go. I know how annoyed Emily gets when I hang out with her and Reed. Two's company and three's a crowd!

"Katie!" Emily stopped me.

I turned in surprise. "Yeah?"

"You look upset." Even though she's my sister, Emily can be really perceptive when she wants to be.

I shrugged off her question. I didn't really want to get into it with her in front of Reed. "It's nothing."

"It's Tante Anne, isn't it?" she persisted.

"Yes," I admitted, sinking down onto a chair next to the couch. "How did you know?"

"I talked to Michel about it," Emily explained. "I don't know what's wrong with Tante Anne — sometimes I can hardly believe she's Jean-Paul's sister! She and Grand-mère treat Noelle like she's a china doll that's going to break. The poor girl doesn't even have a life."

Emily actually looked angry.

I guess I had been so wrapped up in how I felt that I didn't realize other people in the family were affected, too. It sure felt good to know that they saw the situation the same way I did. "I just don't know what to do!" I burst out gratefully. "I really wanted Noelle to go to the dance on Saturday. She helped so much with the publicity, and she and Brian . . ." I hesitated, not wanting to let Emily think we were playing "Love Connection." But it was such a relief to talk to her that I went ahead. "Well, they're kind of friends now, and he really wanted her to come to the dance!"

"I guess you could talk to Mom, but she seems kind of scared of Grand-mère and Tante Anne," Emily pointed out.

"Yeah, I noticed that," I agreed. "Besides, I don't want Mom to have to take sides against Jean-Paul's relatives."

All this time Reed had been shooting pool. But now he straightened up and rested his cue on the edge of the table. I guess he had been listening the whole time. He said, "It sounds like it's the women in this family that are all uptight. Why don't you talk to your uncle and your stepdad? I bet they'll side with you and Noelle."

I had to agree with him. "You're right. Oncle Pierre was going to let Noelle go to Sabrina's in the first place. And at dinner the other night, he told Tante Anne that Noelle should go out and have fun with girls her own age."

Emily nodded.

"Maybe if I could get Jean-Paul to come to the fair and the dance, he can get Tante Anne and Oncle Pierre to come with him." I began to plot. "Then they'll definitely bring Noelle!"

Then I noticed Noelle standing in the corner of the room. She must have walked through the door so quietly that we didn't notice her. She looked like she had tears in her eyes.

"*Merci*, Katie, but it won't help," she said sadly.

I jumped up and caught her by the arm. "Why not?"

"Once Maman has made up her mind, it is no use. You and your family are the nicest people I have ever met, and I thank you for trying to help. But please, just forget about it all. It will only make things worse, believe me." Then Noelle pulled her arm out of my loose grasp and ran out of the room.

I turned to look helplessly at Emily. I had to do something!

After spending practically the whole evening on the phone with Sabrina, we had our plan of attack all ready. When we consulted with Randy and Allison, they both thought we should let Noelle fight her own battles with her mother, but I was sure she would never have the nerve to do that.

I invited Sabs over to our house for the afternoon the next day, which was Friday. We stayed up in my room until we heard Mom's car returning from that day's excursion. Drawing deep breaths to give us courage, Sabrina and I went downstairs. We found Mom, Noelle, Grand-mère, and Tante Anne having tea in the living room.

"Good, they're all in there. I can introduce you to them so you can see what we're up against!" I whispered to Sabrina. I led her into the living room.

"Hi, everybody. I want to introduce you to my best friend, Sabrina Wells." I forced myself to smile at Tante Anne, who wore her usual scowl.

Grand-mère looked Sabrina up and down

critically, like she did with everyone she met. I'm sure she didn't approve of Sabrina's jeans and faded denim shirt with the silver and turquoise buttons on it. She had no idea that the whole outfit was totally in style.

Sabrina sprang right into action. Before I could stop her, she was bombarding Tante Anne.

"Hello, what a pleasure to meet you both! Hello, Mrs. Campbell . . . I mean Mrs. Beauvais. Hi, Noelle. Katie and I were discussing what to wear tomorrow to the fair and the dance. I hope you're all going to be there! It should be really great. Everybody in town is going. Our friend Randy's mom — she's an artist — is entering an ice sculpture in the contest!"

Sabrina paused just for a second to look around and check the reaction from her audience. Mom smiled at her, as usual. Mom really likes Sabrina. And she knows by now that it's best just to let Sabrina talk herself out before you even try to interrupt.

Tante Anne and Grand-mère sat there with eyebrows raised. You could definitely tell that they were mother and daughter.

"So, will you all be there tomorrow?" Sabrina asked hopefully.

I waited for their answer. Finally Grand-mère answered stiffly, "No, I do not believe this fair is for us."

"Oh, well, I understand. It will probably be too much walking for someone of your, um . . . age." Sabrina tried to say it delicately, but it came out sounding pretty blunt. I cringed.

Then Sabrina continued, "But you will let Noelle go, won't you? It will be so much fun!"

"I don't think Noelle will be going either, young lady. I try to keep her away from such common public events," Tante Anne told Sabrina coldly.

I just stood there with my mouth open, feeling the blood rush to my face. Then I glanced at Noelle. Her eyes were open wide in amazement at her mother's rudeness. Mom seemed pretty shocked, too. Sabrina just looked dazed, almost as if she had been struck by Tante Anne physically.

I decided I couldn't take it anymore. "Tante Anne! I know you are a guest in our home, but Sabrina is my friend —"

Then Noelle interrupted me, "Katie, wait! She is my mother and Sabrina is my friend, too."

I looked at her in surprise. Noelle had stood

up and was talking loudly and clearly. She turned to her mother and said, "Maman, I have listened to you for my whole life. But now I must tell you that you are very wrong."

Tante Anne looked horrified at Noelle's bravery. She said something sharply in French.

"Maman! If you wish to speak to me in front of our American friends and relatives, then speak in English!" Noelle told her, her voice shaking slightly.

Sabrina and I looked at each other in astonishment. I didn't know that Noelle had it in her.

White-faced, Tante Anne replied, "Noelle! You have never acted so disrespectfully to me before! This is proof that these vulgar girls have made you forget all the manners I have taught you."

"You have forgotten your manners, Maman! You are rude to my friends and our hostess. You talk in French when you know they cannot understand. You have not said one nice thing to anyone since we have been here!" Noelle cried.

"Noelle!" Grand-mère cried out. She began to fan herself with her napkin like she was having a heart attack or something.

"Look what you've done to your grandmother! Noelle, you will go directly upstairs and pack your bags. We are leaving this place as soon as possible. These *bourgeois* have influenced you enough!" Tante Anne said furiously.

I didn't know what *bourgeois* meant, but I sure didn't like the way she said it. This wasn't turning out at all like Sabrina and I had expected. Noelle just stood there helplessly, and Mom sat frozen in her chair, horrified.

Then a man's voice from the doorway startled us all.

"We are not leaving until Sunday, as planned. What on earth is going on here?" Oncle Pierre asked. He stood frowning in the doorway, with Jean-Paul behind him.

Tante Anne burst out in a wave of French. Oncle Pierre angrily raised one hand to silence her. "We will discuss this in our room in private," he told her firmly. He turned around and left the room.

Tante Anne followed him out of the room, throwing a nasty look toward Sabrina and me. Then Jean-Paul went over to Grand-mère and lifted her out of her chair. "Come, Maman. I will help you up to your room. You should lie down."

Once they had all gone, I nervously said to Mom, "I'm really, really sorry."

She breathed deeply for a second and then said, "No, it's all my fault, Katie. I've tried my best, but I'm afraid Anne and Grand-mère will always look down on me. I'm sure they think I only married Jean-Paul for his money. They've never said so, of course, but the way they treat me, it's very clear."

Now I really felt awful. I knew that this fight over Noelle had nothing to do with Mom, but I guessed that Tante Anne and Grand-mère had intimidated her so badly that she couldn't see things clearly. And instead of being understanding and helping Mom, I had just made things a million times worse!

Then Noelle stepped forward. "You must not think that, Tante Eileen. Maman does not dislike you — she treats everyone that way." Noelle gave us all a sad little smile. "Especially me. Every time I begin to enjoy myself, she finds some way to spoil it."

"Thank you, Noelle. You're very sweet," Mom said, though she didn't sound convinced. "Excuse me." Then she left the room.

Sabrina, Noelle, and I were left alone in the

living room.

"Ohmygosh. I'm so sorry! All I wanted to do was apologize to your mother and convince her to let you go to the fair, and now I've destroyed your whole family!" groaned Sabrina.

Noelle shook her head. "Do not feel bad, Sabrina. I had to stand up to Maman, and I'm glad you helped me do it. *Merci beaucoup!*" Noelle said. "And now I must go and apologize to Grand-mère and Maman. I hope I will see you again before I must go!"

Sabrina nodded helplessly and then gave Noelle a big hug.

After she went upstairs, Sabrina and I stood there alone for a minute. We both felt so bad, we didn't know what to say. Then we heard Michel come in the front door. The minute he looked in and saw our faces, he wanted to know what on earth had been going on. By the time we had finished explaining it all, he looked pretty bummed out, too.

Noelle had been upstairs for almost half an hour when she came bounding down the stairs. "Katie! Sabrina! Michel!" she cried. "Maman and Papa talked it over, and we are staying until

Sunday. I can go to the fair and the dance, too! And Maman apologized to me!"

"What?" I cried in disbelief.

"And I get to move back into your room, Katie!" Noelle went on happily. And she hugged all three of us at once.

Chapter Nine

It was Saturday morning, the day of the Main Street Fair, and Noelle and I were in my room, getting dressed.

"I don't believe it's Saturday already!" I cried. "The fair and the dance are going to be great!"

"*Oui*, except I am sad that we must leave tomorrow," Noelle reminded me.

I nodded my head. "I know." I had to admit, I was going to miss Noelle.

I knew that things still weren't great with Noelle's family. Last night Grand-mère didn't even come down to dinner, and Tante Anne barely spoke to anyone. Oncle Pierre was still friendly to my family, but you could tell he and Tante Anne were having a fight, the way they acted so polite to each other. Even Mom seemed to have given up on acting the good hostess.

Luckily, with Michel around, we didn't have to worry about dinner table conversation. But

even that was awkward, since mostly he chattered about tomorrow's fair. Every time he men-
tioned it, Tante Anne jerked in her chair as if
someone were sticking pins into her.

I sighed and tried to put our family problems
out of my mind.

"Katie, what should I wear?" Noelle asked.
"I've never been to a fair before."

I smiled. "Don't worry, we'll find something.
There's got to be plenty to choose from in all
those suitcases you brought — and if there isn't,
luckily you and I wear just about the same size."
It sure was fun sharing my room and my closet
with my cousin.

Going through Noelle's clothes, we found a
really cute white cotton button-down shirt with
red embroidery on the collar and cuffs. "That's
traditional Swiss embroidery. I bought this in the
town where my school is," Noelle explained. "I
don't think Maman has ever seen it."

"It would go really well with these navy wool
trousers of yours," I pointed out. "You can borrow my red suspenders, and top it off with that
short navy jacket you wore last Sunday. And, oh
— you know what would really make this outfit?"

"No, what?"

"Just wait a minute — I'll show you!" I ran through the bathroom into Michel's room and borrowed his pale-blue-and-crimson paisley silk tie. I remembered him wearing it to the rehearsal dinner for Mom and Jean-Paul's wedding, and I knew it would be perfect for Noelle's outfit today.

When I showed it to Noelle, she looked doubtful. "Maman doesn't even like for me to wear trousers, unless I am skiing," she said. "With the suspenders and the tie, she will tell me that I am dressed like a boy."

"That's the whole idea — kind of a Ralph Lauren look," I explained.

"Who is this Ralph Lauren — did I meet him that day at the mall?" Noelle asked, confused.

"No." I laughed and pulled out *Young Chic*, Sabrina's favorite magazine. Usually I don't read it, but this was a copy she had left over here one day. I was glad I had it now so I could show Noelle the fashion ads, and explain that Ralph Lauren is a popular designer.

While Noelle was getting dressed, I put on a pair of off-white wool tights and a matching turtleneck. Over those, I wore my flared denim mini skirt, a warm oatmeal-colored roll-neck sweater, and my brown suede boots. I didn't look as sophisticated as Noelle, but I figured it was just right for a day at the fair. Noelle stood in front of the mirror, putting her hair up in a french braid. "So, what time are we meeting Sabrina and Randy and Allison?" she asked.

"One o'clock by the pond," I told her. "I don't want to miss the judging for the ice sculptures. I'll bet Randy's mom was there all night finishing hers. Good thing it's cold today so they won't melt!"

Noelle pulled a fluffy white scrunchy onto her braid, then studied her reflection in the full-length mirror on the back of my closet door. "You look great!" I assured her.

Noelle blushed. "Thanks. I only hope Maman doesn't say anything."

"Well, you are dressed perfectly for an outdoor fair," I insisted. "She can't really say anything, since she probably never went to one before!"

Noelle tilted her head to one side and thought about it for a moment. "You are right! Besides, I do love these clothes!"

A little while later, Noelle and I were at Elm Park meeting our friends. The pond was full of skaters and there were crowds of people up and down Main Street. Vendors were busy selling roasted chestnuts, hot dogs, pretzels, popcorn, and hot apple cider.

Noelle's eyes were open wide with excitement the whole time. I was glad she was having a good time. I just wished that Tante Anne and Grand-mère would come out today and enjoy the fair, too. Maybe if they had some fun every once in a while, they wouldn't have to spoil other people's good times. But before I left home, I had made Jean-Paul and Oncle Pierre promise to try and come to the fair, or at least to the dance tonight. Michel had said he would try to convince them to come, too.

Beside the pond, we caught sight of Randy's mother, surrounded by a crowd of people. "Wow, Mrs. Zak! Your sculpture is awesome!" I cried. Randy and Allison had been over to see the finished product early that morning, but this was my first glimpse of it. It was eight feet high and looked exactly like Randy, all the way up to the spiky hair!

Randy's mother smiled and said, "Thank

you. But please, call me Olivia. 'Mrs. Zak' makes me feel old!" She's always telling us that, but I still felt goofy calling a grown-up by her first name.

"Randy! The statue is *magnifique*!" Noelle said.

"I didn't know your mother was going to make it look just like you." I laughed.

"Neither did Randy!" Sabrina giggled.

"She did it from a picture and surprised me," Randy told me. "And boy, was I surprised when I finally saw it this morning!"

"I bet!" I cried.

"Here, let me take a picture of the two of you together — the Ice Randy and the Real Randy!" Allison joked. She was taking pictures of the fair for the school newspaper.

Randy posed with her giant twin, beaming. "I don't know," Sabrina teased as we looked on. "I don't think Acorn Falls is big enough for two Randys!"

The judging wasn't for another hour, so we decided to walk down Main Street and see what else was going on.

We got free samples of apple pie at the bake shop. Fitzie's, the local ice-cream parlor, was selling ice-cream cones for just five cents, which was their everyday price forty-eight years ago, when the first fair was held. A brass band played in the gazebo on the Town Hall green. And next to that, the Rotary Club had set up an old-fashioned carousel that they had rented for the occasion. Noelle begged us to take a ride on it with her, so we did, even though I usually think merry-go-rounds are for little kids. But I have to admit, it was really cool, whizzing around on those beautiful carved wooden horses with their decorated saddles and flowing manes.

But the best part was the banner stretched across Main Street that we had made. Allison, of course, took a picture of it for the school newspaper. "Great," Randy groaned. "Now we're going to be picked to decorate every dance and every fair until we're eighty-five years old!"

We made sure to hurry back to the park in time for the pie-eating contest. Sabrina's twin brother, Sam, and his friends Nick and Arizonna were entered in it, and we wanted to cheer them on. It was a pretty funny sight — I think they got more pie in their hair and noses than in their mouths! Sam ended up the big winner. Sabrina couldn't resist telling him, "I always knew you had the biggest mouth in town, Sam!"

Then we went over to a show being put on by the Chippewa Native American Club. Being a full-blooded Chippewa, Allison knew most of the people there. "They sure look different, though, even to me, when I see them wearing their Chippewa dress," Allison admitted. Some of them were performing traditional tribe dances, and Allison explained to us the significance of each dance. It was really interesting.

"Are there a lot of Native Americans in Canada?" I asked Noelle.

"Yes," she said, nodding, "but not many in Montreal, I think. At least, I don't see them at the places I usually go." Then I remembered what Tante Anne had said about Noelle not going to "common public events." Now I understood how exciting it was for her to mingle with the crowds at the fair.

By now it was time for the judges to announce the winners of the ice sculpture contest. On our way over to the pond, though, we ran into Brian and Scottie. I noticed Noelle blushing.

"Hi, Noelle." Brian smiled. "Remember me?"

"Hello, Brian," Noelle said shyly. But at least this time she looked him in the eyes.

"Are you still going to the barn dance tonight?" he asked.

Noelle nodded.

"Great. Promise to dance with me at least one dance, okay?"

"I promise," Noelle replied, smiling. But then Randy grabbed her arm.

"Come on, you guys, the judges are already making the announcements!" Randy made us hurry along.

When we reached the pond, the crowd was already applauding. Pushing our way through, we saw a big blue ribbon stuck right on the Ice Randy's chest. Mrs. Zak had won first place!

The day seemed to fly by. Before I knew it, the sun was setting and the bonfire was lit beside the pond. Since we had been eating all day long, we really weren't hungry, but we knew we were expected home for dinner before the barn dance.

We were a little late meeting Emily, who had promised to drive us home. By the time we rushed in the front door, it was almost six-thirty. "Dinner's in ten minutes," groaned Emily, "and I still haven't changed for the dance!" Noelle and I grinned at each other. Emily always had to change outfits at least twelve times before she decided what to wear anywhere.

"Let's not change our clothes, Noelle," I suggested. "The barn dance isn't a dress-up kind of occasion. What we're wearing is perfectly fine."

After our fun day at the fair, I was afraid that dinner would be a real comedown. We all sat at the table in silence for a few minutes, while Mrs. Smith served us bowls of soup. Then Jean-Paul said, "So, how was the fair today?"

"We had a good time," I said, trying not to sound too excited. "Randy's mother won first prize in the ice sculpture contest. And Sabrina's brother Sam won the pie-eating contest."

"That's wonderful." Jean-Paul smiled.

"Did you have a good time, Noelle?" Oncle Pierre asked.

"*Oui*," Noelle answered simply, with a sidelong glance at her mother. Tante Anne was looking Noelle's outfit up and down critically.

"Tell me what you saw," Oncle Pierre prompted.

"We rode on an old carousel that had beautiful painted horses," Noelle began slowly. Then the thrill of the day welled up inside her. She went on eagerly, "There was so much food everywhere — I ate hot chestnuts and apple pie and ice cream. Oh, and I saw real live Indians all dressed up and singing and dancing. Do you know that Katie's friend Allison is an American Chippewa Indian?"

Tante Anne let out a "Humph!"

"It all sounds lovely," Oncle Pierre said, ignoring his wife.

"Well, I do hope that you are going to change your clothes before this dance!" Grand-mère interrupted.

Noelle looked down sadly. "I thought I would go like this."

Then, for the first time in a week, Mom actually disagreed with our guests. She said firmly, "Noelle looks absolutely adorable in that outfit!"

"Especially in my tie," Michel joked.

"I love what you're wearing, Noelle! Do you think I should wear my other skirt?" Emily said, uncertainly.

We all continued to talk. Grand-mère and Tante Anne were outnumbered.

"I would love to see this barn dance tonight!" Oncle Pierre said.

"*Oui*! I think we should all go. I've never been to a barn dance. And I haven't been out dancing with Eileen for a while," Jean-Paul said with a smile.

"I think it would be great if you guys all came! It's going to be a lot of fun. Sabrina's parents are coming!" I cried.

Tante Anne shook her head firmly. "We must pack our bags, and we should get to bed early," she said. "We have our trip home tomorrow."

"Nonsense, that's not until tomorrow afternoon. And the flight home only takes an hour and a half," Oncle Pierre contradicted her.

"Mrs. Smith can pack for you," Jean-Paul suggested.

"We will see!" Tante Anne said, ending the topic for the rest of the meal. Somehow I had a feeling that they wouldn't be coming to the dance tonight.

But at least Noelle could go — that was the most important thing.

Before long, we were walking into the barn. There was quite a crowd gathered already.

Noelle looked up at the hundreds of tiny white lights suspended from the ceiling like stars. "Oh, Katie! It is so wonderful!"

I nodded and looked around at the bales of hay stacked along the walls, the long table covered with punch bowls and cookies, and the musicians standing on a big wagon at the end of the barn, tuning up their fiddles.

"Come on! I see Sabrina, Randy, and Allison," I cried. Even in a crowd, it's always easy to pick out Allison's dark head, since she's the tallest girl in our class.

Just as we met them, the band struck up a Western song and people began to dance.

"Hello, ladies!" Brian said, walking up behind Noelle. Scottie was with him.

"*Bon soir!*" Noelle smiled and then blushed.

"Come on! Let's dance!" Brian grabbed Noelle's hand.

She looked at me and I said, "Go on!"

Noelle smiled and then let Brian lead her out to the dance floor. Scottie bowed jokingly and said, "May I have this dance?"

I giggled and said, "Yes!"

Soon everybody was dancing and having a great time. We had enough people in our group to form our own square, with some extra dancers to fill in whenever anyone got tired. Sabrina danced with Nick and then with Michel. Allison was partners with Billy Dixon, a guy she tutors in math. And Randy danced with Arizonna. He also moved here not so long ago, so that gives them something in common.

Finally the band took a break. We all went to the punch table to cool down. I had forgotten what hard work square dancing is!

Noelle's eyes were shining as she chatted with Brian. I nudged Sabrina and whispered, "It looks like they're getting along very well!"

"I knew it!" Sabrina agreed. Then, turning her head, she gasped and grabbed my hand. "Oh-mygosh! Look who just walked in!"

I spun around and looked at the large open doorway. There stood Mom, Jean-Paul, Oncle Pierre, Tante Anne, and even Grand-mère!

Chapter Ten

"I don't believe it! They really came!" I cried. Noelle turned to see what Sabrina and I were looking at. Her mouth dropped open in shock.

Jean-Paul caught sight of us and waved. Then he took Grand-mère's arm and led her into the room. I could tell by the look on Grand-mère and Tante Anne's faces that they weren't exactly happy to be here.

"Bon soir!" Jean-Paul greeted us. Then the band began to play again. Jean-Paul took Grand-mère's arm and pulled her toward the dance floor. "Come on, Maman. Dance with your son!"

Grand-mère looked really surprised, but before she could say anything, Jean-Paul had swept her into the crowd of dancers.

Oncle Pierre's eyes looked bright and mischievous. "Let's dance, *ma chère!*" he said to Tante Anne.

Tante Anne tried to protest, but she had no choice.

Reed and Emily were already on the dance floor. They trotted over to dance with Jean-Paul, Grand-mère, Pierre, and Tante Anne. Then Michel tapped my mom on the shoulder. "They need one more couple to form their square," he pointed out. "Would you like to dance, Mom?" Even though Emily and I still don't feel comfortable calling Jean-Paul "Dad," Michel likes to call our mother "Mom."

She smiled. "I'd love to."

Noelle watched her mother and father dancing, in amazement. When the song was over, Grand-mère was out of breath but smiling from ear to ear. Tante Anne and Oncle Pierre went right on dancing, and Michel and Grand-mère danced together, so Mom and Jean-Paul could, too.

I whispered to Noelle, "I knew everything would turn out okay."

Noelle smiled and gave me a big hug. "Thank you, Katie! All this would have never happened if it wasn't for you."

"Hold it — don't move!" Allison snapped a picture of the two of us. Then she thrust the camera at Arizonna and said, "Now get all five of us!"

Allison, Randy, Sabs, Noelle, and I all hugged each other as Arizonna took the picture.

"Okay, enough photography! I want to dance with Noelle," Brian demanded, and he and Noelle were off again.

The evening was a real hit. We all danced and laughed and had a great time. Even Tante Anne and Grand-mère looked happy, although they didn't say so out loud!

When we got home, Noelle and I whispered about the dance for almost an hour in the dark in my room. When I finally fell asleep, I could still hear the music in my head. I dreamed of dancing and stars all night.

The next morning when I woke up, though, I found Noelle in the closet packing her suitcase. Sadly, I remembered that today was the day that she had to go home. But I was determined to make our last few hours together happy. I jumped out of bed and headed for the shower, still humming a tune from the square dance. "I'll be out in a minute, and then I'll help you finish packing!" I told her.

While we were packing up Noelle's things, we went over all the details of the dance once again. I even got Noelle to admit that she liked Brian, and that she had agreed to write him once she got back to her school.

Randy, Sabrina, and Allison had promised to come over around eleven o'clock to say good-bye to Noelle. It was already ten-thirty, so we wanted to finish packing now. We did one last search around the room to make sure Noelle hadn't forgotten anything. Then we snapped shut all of her suitcases and carried them down the hall to the elevator. Usually, I never use the elevator, since the back stairs are closer to my bedroom. But with all those suitcases, today I was really glad we had an elevator!

At the other end of the hall, Tante Anne and Oncle Pierre were already waiting for the elevator.

"Good morning," I greeted them.

"Katie! Noelle! Good morning," Oncle Pierre said with his usual cheerfulness.

"Good morning," Tante Anne said. Something seemed a little different about her today. I wouldn't say she was friendly or anything, but she didn't have the usual mean look on her face. And I noticed that she and Oncle Pierre were actually holding hands!

Downstairs in the dining room, Grand-mère was sitting with Jean-Paul and Mom drinking coffee and talking about last night.

Michel, as usual, was wolfing down a huge stack of pancakes smothered in maple syrup.

"*Eh bien*, Jean-Paul. I don't know how long it's been since I danced like that," Grand-mère was saying.

"*Oui, Maman.* You look thirty years younger," Jean-Paul teased her.

"I felt it!" Grand-mère replied, and she actually smiled. Then, when she saw Noelle and me walk in, she said, "Noelle, that was a very handsome boy you were dancing with last night." Noelle blushed. And Grand-mère added, "He was almost as cute as Katie's little boyfriend." I guess she had to mean Scottie! Now it was my turn to blush.

Michel pointed at me with his syrupy fork and snickered. "Your little boyfriend!" he repeated.

I jabbed him in the shoulder and hissed, "Scottie is not my boyfriend!" Then I noticed Jean-Paul and Mom smiling at each other. I knew they weren't laughing at me, though. They were just happy that, finally, Grand-mère was acting like a normal nosy grandmother, and Tante Anne and Oncle Pierre weren't fighting anymore!

We finished eating just as the doorbell rang. Noelle looked up excitedly. "That's probably the girls!" she guessed.

"Why don't you go let them in?" I suggested. "I have to finish my pancakes." Knowing what my friends had been planning, I wanted Noelle to open the door herself.

I was watching from the other side of the foyer when Noelle opened the front door. Sabrina stood there with a big sign that said: BON VOYAGE, NOELLE! Randy and Allison were behind her, both holding packages wrapped in pretty purple paper.

"Surprise!" Sabrina, Randy, and Allison cried and marched inside.

Noelle gasped in delight and exclaimed, "You are all wonderful!"

"Come on into the family room. Noelle can open her presents there," I told them and led the way.

"Presents? That was not necessary," Noelle protested.

"Just open them," Sabrina said laughing.

"This one first!" Randy said, thrusting the

one she was holding at Noelle.

"Okay!" Noelle smiled. She sat on the couch in the family room and carefully unwrapped the package.

"Oh, this is wonderful!" she cried and held up the picture of the five of us at the dance last night. It was framed in a clear plastic frame.

"How did you get it developed so soon?" she asked.

"Obviously, the girl has never heard of one-hour photo stores," Randy teased her. "The one at the mall was open at nine this morning."

I laughed.

"Now this one!" Allison said and handed Noelle the other present.

Noelle placed the picture carefully on the coffee table and began to open the second gift.

As soon as the paper was half off, Sabrina couldn't contain herself any longer. "It's an address book," she blurted out. "And we wrote all of our addresses in it. I think even Brian's address is in there!" Sabrina gave us a wink as Noelle blushed and flipped through the book.

"And you have to promise to write," Allison added firmly.

"Oh, I will! *Merci beaucoup!*" Noelle cried, her

eyes looking misty.

"Wait, Michel and I have something for you too," I told her. I ran back into the dining room, where Michel were devouring his third helping of pancakes. "Where did you hide the present?" I asked him.

"What present?" he asked, frowning.

"Remember, I whispered to you at the fair yesterday to buy it for Noelle. I even slipped you some money. You promised you'd buy it, and you said you'd wrap it up, too!" I began to get angry. Then I noticed Michel grinning.

"Relax, K.C.," he said. "It's in the hall closet."

He showed me where he had hidden the box, which was wrapped pretty neatly, considering Michel's usual messy presents. Then he followed me back into the family room.

Noelle eagerly opened the box. Inside was an extralarge white T-shirt that said: ACORN FALLS 48TH ANNUAL MAIN STREET FAIR.

"Do you like it?" Michel asked.

"*Oui! Merci beaucoup!*" Noelle cried, and stood up and hugged Michel and me.

"I have made so many new friends! It is very hard to leave. I don't have many real friends at home," Noelle said sadly.

"But we'll still be your friends. And you have to come visit us again real soon," Sabrina insisted.

"And we can come visit you," Michel suggested.

"Look at it this way — now we all have a new pen pal in Switzerland!" Allison said brightly.

"*Oui!*" Noelle agreed.

Then we all hugged her at once. I felt especially warm inside, because I knew that not only did I have a new cousin, but now I had a new friend, too.

Don't Miss
GIRL TALK #40
SABRINA WINS BIG!

"Does anybody have a pen?"

I didn't look up to see if anyone was listening. It was chaos here in the Wells residence— there must have been about ten kids sprawled out in the living room. I'm Sabrina Wells, by the way. It was almost four thirty-five on a Saturday afternoon and I was running out of time. I had less than half an hour to get my Totally Teen Fantasy Sweepstakes entry into the mail. It had to go out by five o'clock. That's the last time they pick up mail on Saturday in Acorn Falls. It's one of the drawbacks of living in a small town in Minnesota. If I mailed it on Sunday, my entry wouldn't be postmarked until Monday. And then I'd be disqualified.

"Does anyone have a black pen that works?" I called out, frantically shaking my ballpoint. "Mine's all out of ink."

"I'll get one," my friend Allison Cloud said, looking up from the book she was reading.

"Check my dad's desk," I suggested.

I was really glad when Allison got up to

help because no one else was paying much attention to me. I guess it's because the Totally Teen Fantasy Sweepstakes is about the twentieth contest I've entered in the past six months. I guess nobody believes that a twelve-year-old girl could ever win a national sweepstakes. But I know I'll get a lucky break someday.

"Here's a blue one. There's no black," Al announced, throwing me a new pen.

I was kneeling at the coffee table trying to get my entry form together. The Totally Teen Fantasy Sweepstakes is a big contest, so everything was taking twice as long as I thought it would. The contest bulletin was long, as usual. But I love reading contest bulletins because they put my name in big letters across the top. It makes me feel like a star. I know the contest bulletin's done by computer and everyone gets the same one, but I still love reading it.

This one said: MISS SABRINA WELLS COULD SOON BE $5,000 RICHER! That was great. But the sentence I liked best read: MISS SABRINA WELLS HAS A ONE-IN-TEN CHANCE OF BECOMING A WINNER. A one-in-ten chance. That didn't sound too hard to me.

**LOOK FOR THE AWESOME GIRL TALK BOOKS IN
A STORE NEAR YOU!**

Fiction
 #1 WELCOME TO JUNIOR HIGH!
 #2 FACE-OFF!
 #3 THE NEW YOU
 #4 REBEL, REBEL
 #5 IT'S ALL IN THE STARS
 #6 THE GHOST OF EAGLE MOUNTAIN
 #7 ODD COUPLE
 #8 STEALING THE SHOW
 #9 PEER PRESSURE
#10 FALLING IN LIKE
#11 MIXED FEELINGS
#12 DRUMMER GIRL
#13 THE WINNING TEAM
#14 EARTH ALERT!
#15 ON THE AIR
#16 HERE COMES THE BRIDE
#17 STAR QUALITY
#18 KEEPING THE BEAT
#19 FAMILY AFFAIR
#20 ROCKIN' CLASS TRIP
#21 BABY TALK
#22 PROBLEM DAD
#23 HOUSE PARTY
#24 COUSINS
#25 HORSE FEVER
#26 BEAUTY QUEENS
#27 PERFECT MATCH
#28 CENTER STAGE
#29 FAMILY RULES
#30 THE BOOKSHOP MYSTERY
#31 IT'S A SCREAM!
#32 KATIE'S CLOSE CALL
#33 RANDY AND THE *PERFECT* BOY

MORE GIRL TALK TITLES TO LOOK FOR

Nonfiction

ASK ALLIE 101 answers to your questions about boys, friends, family, and school!

YOUR PERSONALITY QUIZ Fun, easy quizzes to help you discover the real you!

BOYTALK: HOW TO TALK TO YOUR FAVORITE GUY